The Curious Story of Sean The Zebra
By Dermot Ryan

This is a story about some very special horses who live in a faraway land, in a valley filled with plants, flowers and trees. Their home is called Paradise Ranch. It is an amazing place.

PARADISE
RANCH

Many interesting horses live at Paradise Ranch, not least the black-and-white zebra known as Sean. He is a wacky, wild zebra and the other horses love him. He is funny, always ready to entertain his friends and he is very good at imitating their voices. If you close your eyes and just listen, the zebra could make you think he is one of the other horses at the ranch.

One day, Sean was walking through the farm with his friend, Yankee the Rancher. He was making her laugh as he performed endless impressions of her friends. She laughed and laughed as the zany zebra changed his voice to sound like Archie, the scruffy rag-and-bone horse.

'Oh Sean, you are so funny. You make me so happy; I love being with you. Have you always been this way?' Yankee said.

'Not always,' answered the zebra. 'When I was in my homeland in Africa, I had many problems. There were other animals that wanted to eat me, there were people who wanted to hunt me and there were other strange creatures that wanted to both hunt and eat me!'

Yankee was fascinated. She didn't know anything about Sean's life before Paradise. 'You must tell me more about your life in Africa.'

Sean shuffled his hooves, swished his tail and agreed to tell his story, but he warned her that it was a sad and scary one.

'Be prepared to hold my hoof, dear Yankee; my tale is a frightening one. I am going to tell you about one of the most terrifying creatures in the whole world. He lived in the darkest jungle in deepest Africa and was known as the "Red-Faced Giant".

He was like a human but he was huge. He was taller than the biggest tree in the jungle – so tall that his head always burst through the leaves.

'He lived in a vast underground cavern where it was cool and he was protected from the heat of the sun. The Red-Faced Giant hated the sun because his huge face got burnt every time he went outside. The sun's bright rays shone on his face and made it redder and redder and redder. As his face got hotter and hotter, his mood became angrier and angrier, and when the Red-Faced Giant was angry, every animal in the jungle knew they had to be very careful.

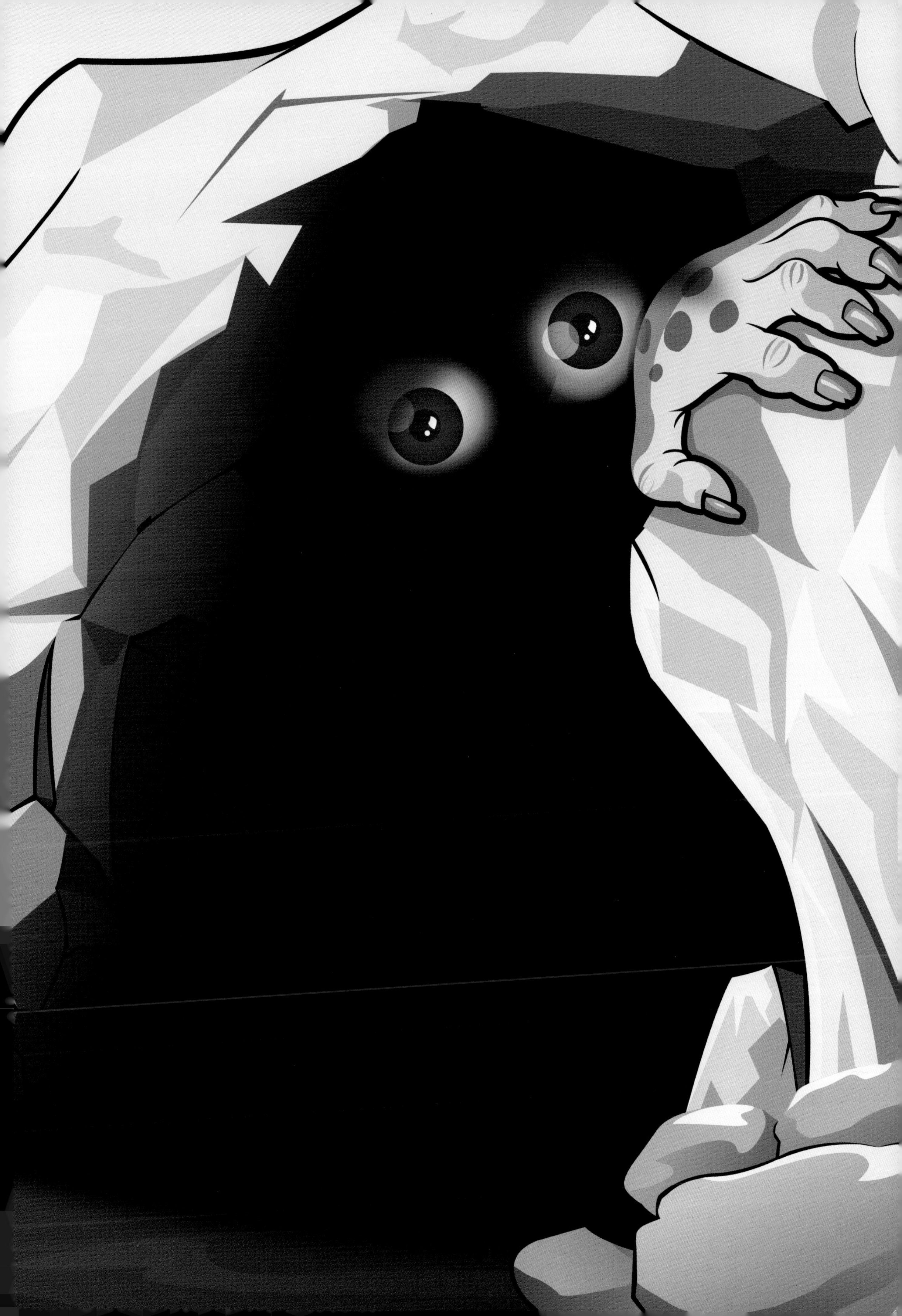

'He was most angry when he was hungry, and unfortunately, because of his size, he was always ravenous. He liked to eat all the animals of the jungle. He spared none. He was strong enough to pick up the biggest elephant and swallow him in one go. However, elephant wasn't his favourite dish – his ideal food was zebra!

'I always avoided going into the big jungle as it was much safer in the open, and the giant could not stand the heat for too long. This suited me, as I preferred to run across the wide open plains of Africa. The problem was that the giant loved the taste of zebra so much, he would sometimes leave the shaded jungle and roam into the open grasslands.

'He knew he didn't have much time to catch his dinner before his face began to sizzle and burn so he was always determined and vicious. Normally, all of the animals ran and just hoped that the heat would become too unbearable for him before he caught them.

'Well, one day I was out grazing. It was a beautiful day: the sun was shining and the birds were singing. Suddenly the sky was full of birds flying away from the jungle. I knew this was a sign that the giant had woken up. When the giant stirred, he needed to eat, and that meant danger for every animal. The monkeys screeched, the lions roared, the crocodiles snarled, and all started to run to their hiding places. They didn't want to end up in a giant tummy.

'All my fellow zebras started to run too, but I decided it was too early. I wanted to wait until he was closer, save my energy and then flee. I waited, but I was very frightened.

'"Boom!" I heard the sound of his footsteps as he approached. The ground moved and shuddered as his massive feet hit the ground. "Boom!" He was getting closer. I could hear and feel his loud, wheezing breath. He sucked the air into his giant lungs and made a deafening screeching sound. Still I waited.

'"Boom!" He took another step. "Boom!" The ground shook. "Boom!" I could see his huge frame. I could smell his awful breath. It was time to run!

'The secret was to run quickly and suddenly. In one giant stride, he could cover a mile so you could never outrun him. If you ran in just one direction, he would swipe you up. You had to change direction often, darting this way and that.

'He was close to me now, and his huge hand came down. I moved and managed to get away, and my tail slid through his fingers. Enormous beads of sweat fell from his face and onto my back, almost drowning me. I swam through the sweat and turned right, left and right again as he swiped once more. He missed, and his giant stride took him away from me and into the distance.

'It was so close – too close. I could no longer live like this; I needed to get away and find a safer place to live. I had heard of a wonderful place where horses lived together in harmony. I travelled across continents, rivers and mountains, searching for Paradise Ranch. Then one day, in the distance, I saw a large horse ploughing a field. He looked so calm and happy. He saw me too and cantered over.

PARADISE
RANCH

'"Do you need food and shelter, my friend?" asked the kind plough horse. "Come with me. Your troubles are over. You have reached Paradise."'

Sean stopped speaking, and Yankee the Rancher found that she couldn't stop crying, she was so surprised by Sean's story. He had always seemed to be such a happy zebra.

'I am very proud of you, Sean. That was a very scary story. We are so lucky to have you with us on the ranch.'

'I am so happy to be here, Yankee. This is the best place in the whole, wide world.'

The End.

Frederick The Racehorse

Alfie The Horse

Louise

Archie The Rag and Bone Horse

Doris The Donkey

Vera The Show Jumper

Michael The Mule

Yankee The Rancher

Connor The Colt

Martin The Show Pony

Joe and Emily

Sean The Zebra

Also available in this series from
www.alfiethehorse.com

/alfiethehorse